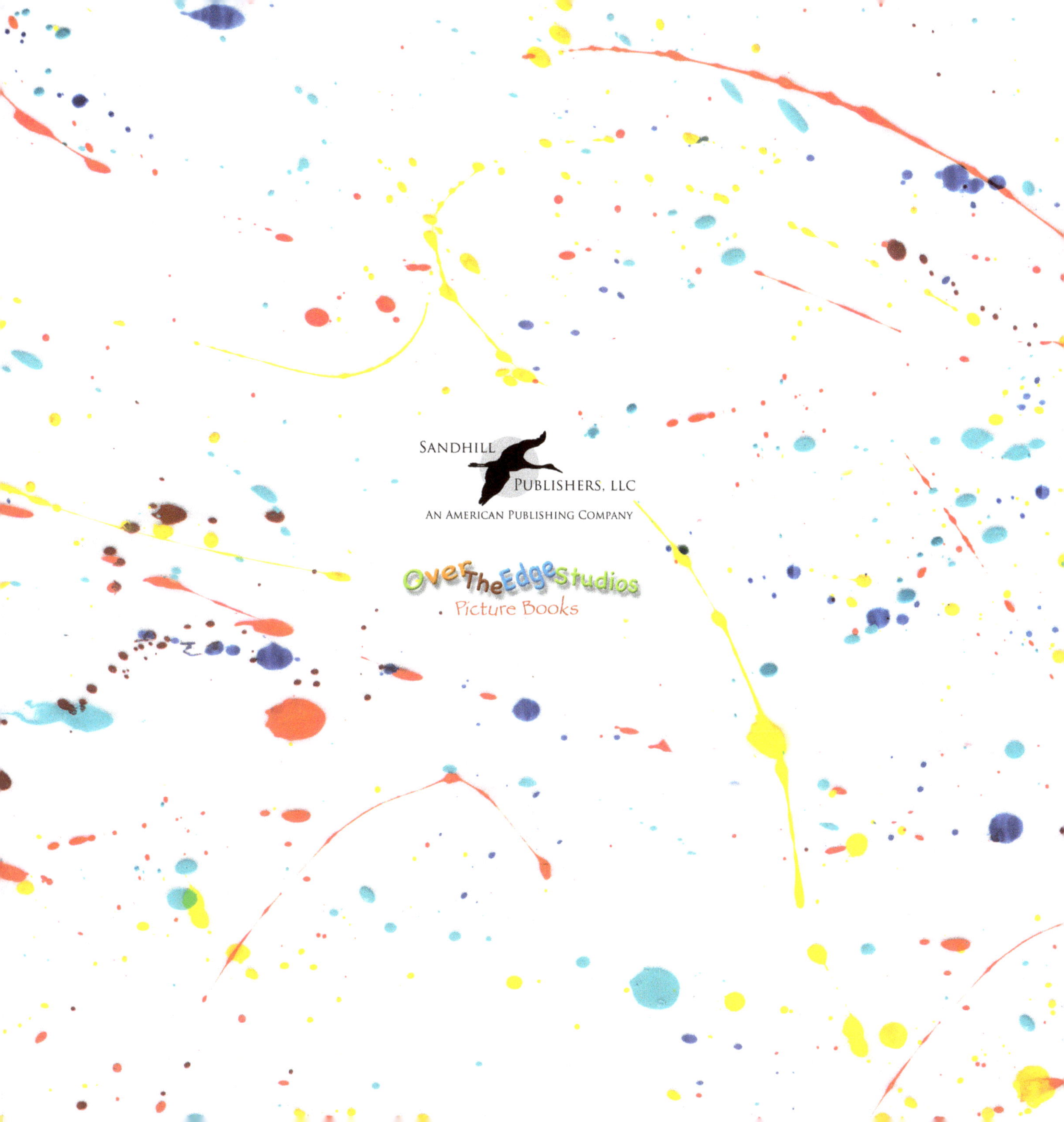

SANDHILL
PUBLISHERS, LLC
AN AMERICAN PUBLISHING COMPANY
OverTheEdgeStudios
Picture Books

For
Jenny and her sweet baby Audrey Sue Ann — T.C.

First Edition/Hardcover

SANDHILL
PUBLISHERS, LLC
AN AMERICAN PUBLISHING COMPANY

Publisher & Registered LLC Agent, Andrew B. Simms

Nashville, Indiana

Contact: sandhillpublishers.com

Illustrations:
Black Line Art: Graphite on tracing paper. • Colored Art: Pastels on tracing paper. • Splatter Paint: Acrylic on tracing paper.
Color Font Accents: Colored pencil on tracing paper. • Digitally composited: Digital color highlights.

Typeface:
Arial Black and Microsoft Himalaya

OverTheEdgeStudios Children's Divsion of Sandhill Publishers

Book design and illustrations by: T. C. Bartlett ®© 2024 • All rights reserved.

Summary: A spunky little girl gives the reader tasks they must perform in preparation for bedtime.

Website • tcbartlett.com

Printed in the United Sates of America

Library of Congress Control Number: 2020937450

ISBN-13: 978-1-7339086-8-9

ISBN-10: 1-7339086-8-4

YOU
HAVE TO DO
WHAT
I SAY!
By
T. C. BARTLETT
OverTheEdgeStudios
Picture Books

My name is Audrey.
And this is my book.
Soooo, you HAVE to do what I say!

My book has three rules.

Rule #1
You have to brush your teeth.

Rule #2
You have to wear your PJ's.

Rule #3
You have to read my book at night,
in your living room,
just before bedtime.

If you don't do what I say,
you can't read my book!

Did you brush your teeth?

Are you in your living room?

Are you wearing your PJ's?

If you're ready to read my book,
you have to say,

yes!

That's not loud enough!
Say yes
LOUDER!

LOUDER!

Now, pat your head five times
and count,
one,
two,
three,
four,
five!

That's
not
fast enough!
Pat
your
Head
Faster!
(Hey! Don't forget to count to five!)
one, two, three, four, five!

That was fun.
You made me smile!

On the count of three,
hold your breath!
One,
two,
three!

Hold
it!

Hold
it!

Breathe!
Breathe!
Breathe!
Breathe!

Now, stand up . . .

Are you standing?
Are you
really
standing?

Then sit down!

Just kidding!
You need to stand up.
I MEAN it!
You have to stand up!

Walk as quietly as a mouse
to your bedroom
and
get
in
bed!
Once you're in bed,
you can read the rest of my book....

MY
BOOK

Are you in bed?

Are you
really
in bed?

Me, too!

Pick your nose!
NO!
STOP!
Don't pick your nose.
That's gross!

You have to say,
"I need a hug!"

Now,
get cozy under your covers.
And say,
"Good night!"

That's too loud!

Say good night again,

but say it in a whisper . . .

Say, "I love you."

. . . I love you, too . . .

Hidden deep in the woods of Brown County, Indiana,
T. C. Bartlett writes and draws his delightful
and heartfelt picture books.

SANDHILL
PUBLISHERS, LLC
AN AMERICAN PUBLISHING COMPANY
OverTheEdgeStudios
Picture Books

www.ingramcontent.com/pod-product-compliance
Lightning Source LLC
Chambersburg PA
CBHW041156300726
48981CB00004B/273